WITHDRAWN

21st Century
Basic Skills
Library

KIDS CAN MAKE MANNERS COUNT
PLAN AHEAD!

by Katie Marsico

Cherry Lake Publishing • Ann Arbor, Michigan

3

Published in the United States of America
by Cherry Lake Publishing
Ann Arbor, Michigan
www.cherrylakepublishing.com

Content Adviser: Tonia Bock, PhD, Associate Professor of Psychology,
University of St. Thomas, St. Paul, Minnesota

Photo Credits: Cover and pages 1, 4, 6, 8, and 10, ©Denise Mondloch;
page 12, ©Simone van den Berg/Shutterstock, Inc.; page 14, ©matka_
Wariatka/Shutterstock, Inc.; page 16, ©Jason Swalwell/Shutterstock,
Inc.; page 18, ©vipman/Shutterstock, Inc.; page 20, ©Sue Harper/
Dreamstime.com

Library of Congress Cataloging-in-Publication Data
Marsico, Katie, 1980–
  Plan ahead! / by Katie Marsico.
     p. cm. — (21st century basic skills library) (Kids can make manners
count)
  Includes bibliographical references and index.
  ISBN 978-1-61080-436-3 (lib. bdg.) — ISBN 978-1-61080-523-0 (e-book) —
ISBN 978-1-61080-610-7 (pbk.)
1. Children—Time management—Juvenile literature. 2. Time
management—Juvenile literature. 3. Etiquette for children and
teenagers—Juvenile literature. I. Title.
  BF637.T5M27 2013
  395.1'22—dc23   2012001710

Cherry Lake Publishing would like to acknowledge
the work of The Partnership for 21st Century Skills.
Please visit www.21stcenturyskills.org for more information.

Printed in the United States of America
Corporate Graphics Inc.
July 2012
CLFA11

TABLE OF CONTENTS

Trouble Finding Time

Kim helped her grandma at the store every Thursday.

One Monday Kim learned she had to do a book report. It was due on Friday.

She waited to start working on the report.

Kim still had not started the report by Thursday. She became worried.

She told her grandma she could not work at the store.

Kim's grandma looked like Kim had let her down.

Making Manners Work

Kim wanted to get an A on her report.

She hated to let her grandma down, though.

Luckily her grandma had a few ideas for Kim.

Kim listened to her grandma talk about planning ahead.

She said it was important to be **organized**.

Being organized was one way to show good **manners**.

Kim's grandma told her she should always plan ahead.

Waiting until the last minute created problems.

Projects had to be done in a hurry. Her teacher might give her a bad grade.

Saved by a Schedule

Kim thought of a few ways to plan ahead.

She could lay out her clothes the night before school.

She could pack her lunch ahead of time, too.

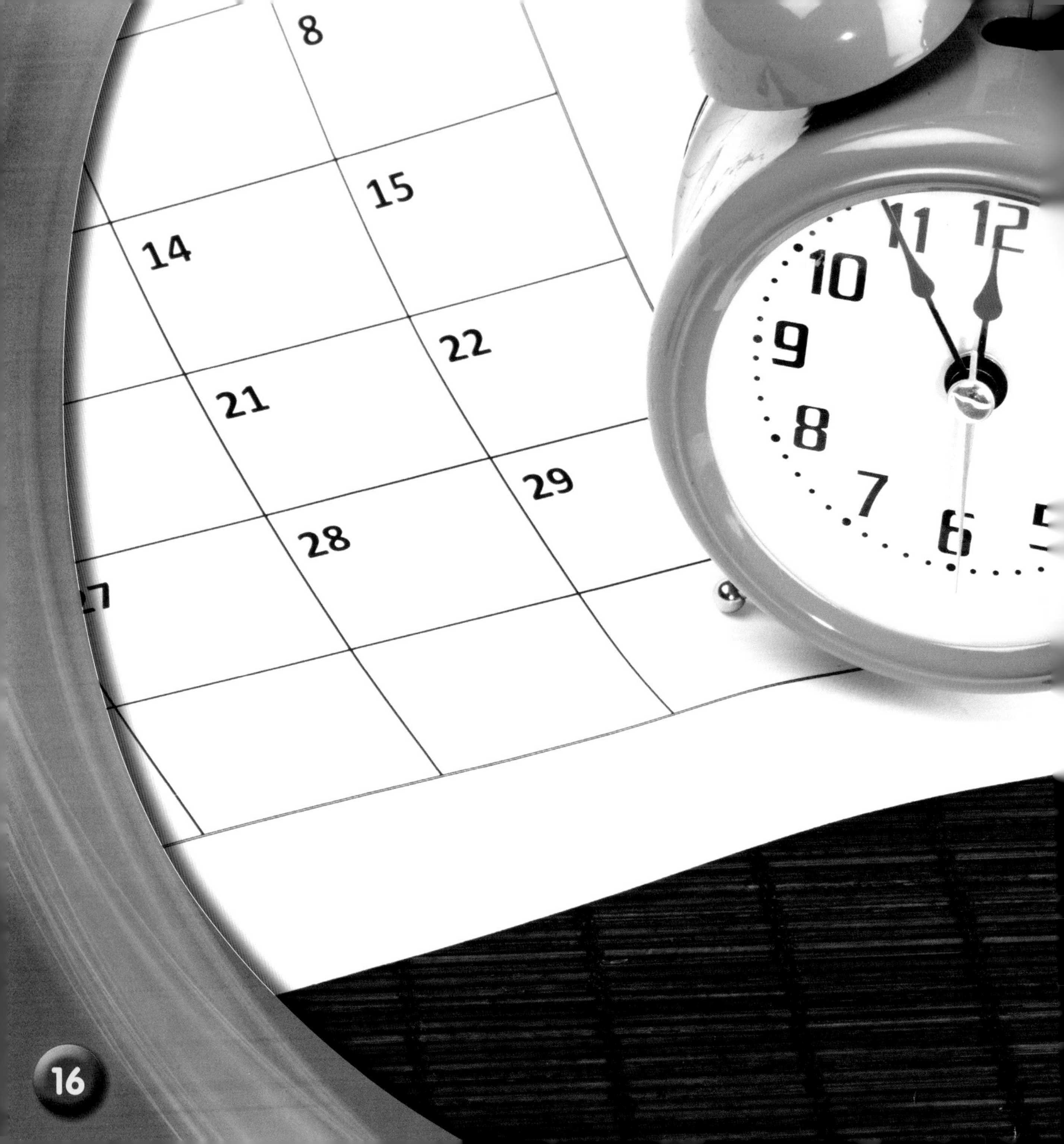

Kim decided to create a **schedule** for herself.

She set aside time for homework every day.

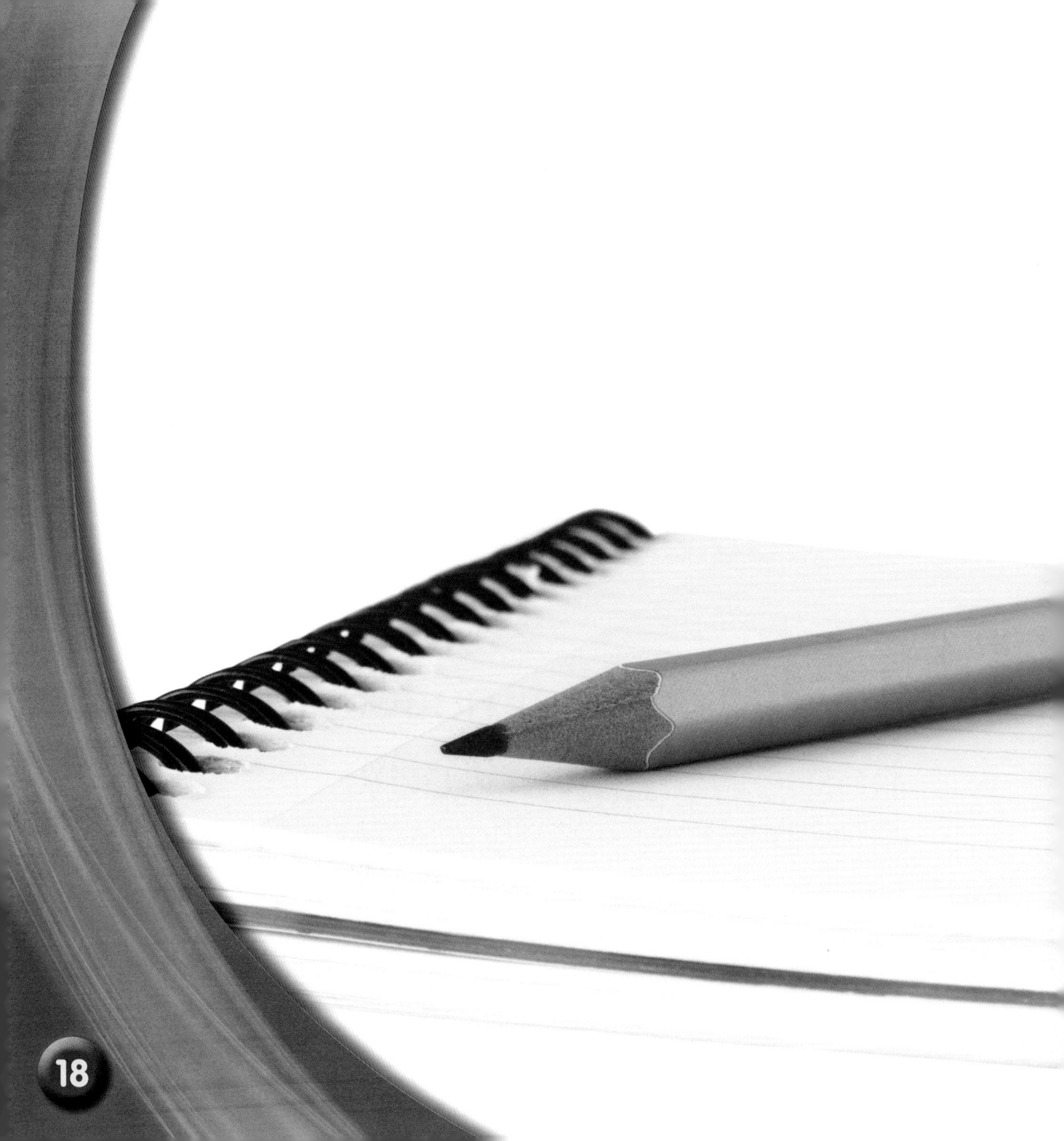

Kim wrote down activities such as working with her grandma.

She would stop putting off her **responsibilities** until Thursdays.

School Report Card

Student Name:	
Subject	
Mathematics	A
Science	A
...nguage	A

Kim started using her schedule to plan ahead.

Soon she stopped worrying about getting everything done.

She earned good grades and made time for her grandma!

Find Out More

BOOK

Chancellor, Deborah. *Good Manners*. New York: Crabtree
  Publishing Company, 2010.

WEB SITE

**U.S. Department of Health and Human Services—
Building Blocks: Manners Quiz**

*www.bblocks.samhsa.gov/family/activities/quizzes/manners.
aspx*

Take a fun online quiz to test how much you know about
manners!

Glossary

manners (MA-nurz) behavior that is kind and polite

organized (OR-guh-nyzed) having activities planned in an
orderly way

responsibilities (ri-spahn-suh-BIL-i-teez) activities that must
be completed

schedule (SKEJ-ool) a plan for doing something at a certain
date and time

Home and School Connection

Use this list of words from the book to help your child become a better reader. Word games and writing activities can help beginning readers reinforce literacy skills.

a	day	helped	making	saved	to
"A"	decided	her	manners	schedule	told
about	do	herself	might	school	too
activities	done	homework	minute	set	trouble
ahead	down	hurry	Monday	she	until
always	due	ideas	night	should	using
an	earned	important	not	show	waited
and	every	in	of	soon	waiting
aside	everything	it	off	start	wanted
as	few	Kim	on	started	was
at	finding	Kim's	one	still	way
bad	for	last	organized	stop	ways
be	Friday	lay	out	stopped	with
before	get	learned	pack	store	work
being	getting	let	plan	such	working
became	give	like	planning	talk	worried
book	good	listened	problems	teacher	worrying
by	grade	looked	projects	the	would
clothes	grades	luckily	putting	Thursday	wrote
could	grandma	lunch	report	Thursdays	
create	had	made	responsibilities	thought	
created	hated	make	said	time	

23

Index

About the Author

Katie Marsico is an author of children's and young-adult reference books. She lives outside of Chicago, Illinois, with her husband and children.